Postman Pat® the Magician

SIMON AND SCHUSTER

Pat picked up the mail from the Greendale Post Office. "There's a package for you, Pat!" said Mrs Goggins.

"Ah, good! My book of magic tricks! It's Meera's birthday party tomorrow and I'm the surprise magician!"

Pat delivered Meera's birthday cards.

"Are you coming to my party, Pat?" she asked. "Mum couldn't find a magician, but there'll be a disco!"

"I'll be there!" Pat winked at Nisha.

"All set, Pat?" whispered Nisha.

"Oh yes! With Ted and Ajay's help, it'll be grand!" Pat grinned.

Pat, Ted and Ajay studied Pat's Magic Book.

"How about this?" Pat suggested. "The Box of Mystery: make your friends disappear right before your eyes!"

"We could make one, couldn't we, Ajay?" said Ted.

"Oh, aye!" nodded Ajay.

"And look. I could get Meera to float up in the air!"

"With a plank of wood and a car jack!" chuckled Ted.

Sara was busy sewing sequins onto Pat's spare uniform, while Julian made a magician's top hat. Jess wasn't being much help. First he splattered paint everywhere . . .

And then he jumped onto the table, getting himself covered with glittery stars and moons.

"Come here, Jess," laughed Pat, arriving back home.

Julian peeled a star off his tail.

"Miaow!"

"Right!" said Pat. "Time to practise my tricks. Pick a card, Julian. Don't let me see it. Now put it back in the pack."

"Your card was . . . the two of spades!"

"No it wasn't, Dad!"

Pat groaned. "I'd better read the instructions again."

"Are you sure you're going to be ready in time, Pat?" asked Sara.

"I've got to be!" Pat grimaced.

Pat worked on his tricks late into the night.

He shuffled the cards and dropped them. He tapped his magic wand and nothing happened.

"Oh dear. Everything's going wrong."

He tried again. This time he shuffled perfectly . . .

. . . and when he tapped the wand, a bunch of flowers appeared.

"Hey presto!" he said happily. "And now I'd better get some sleep!"

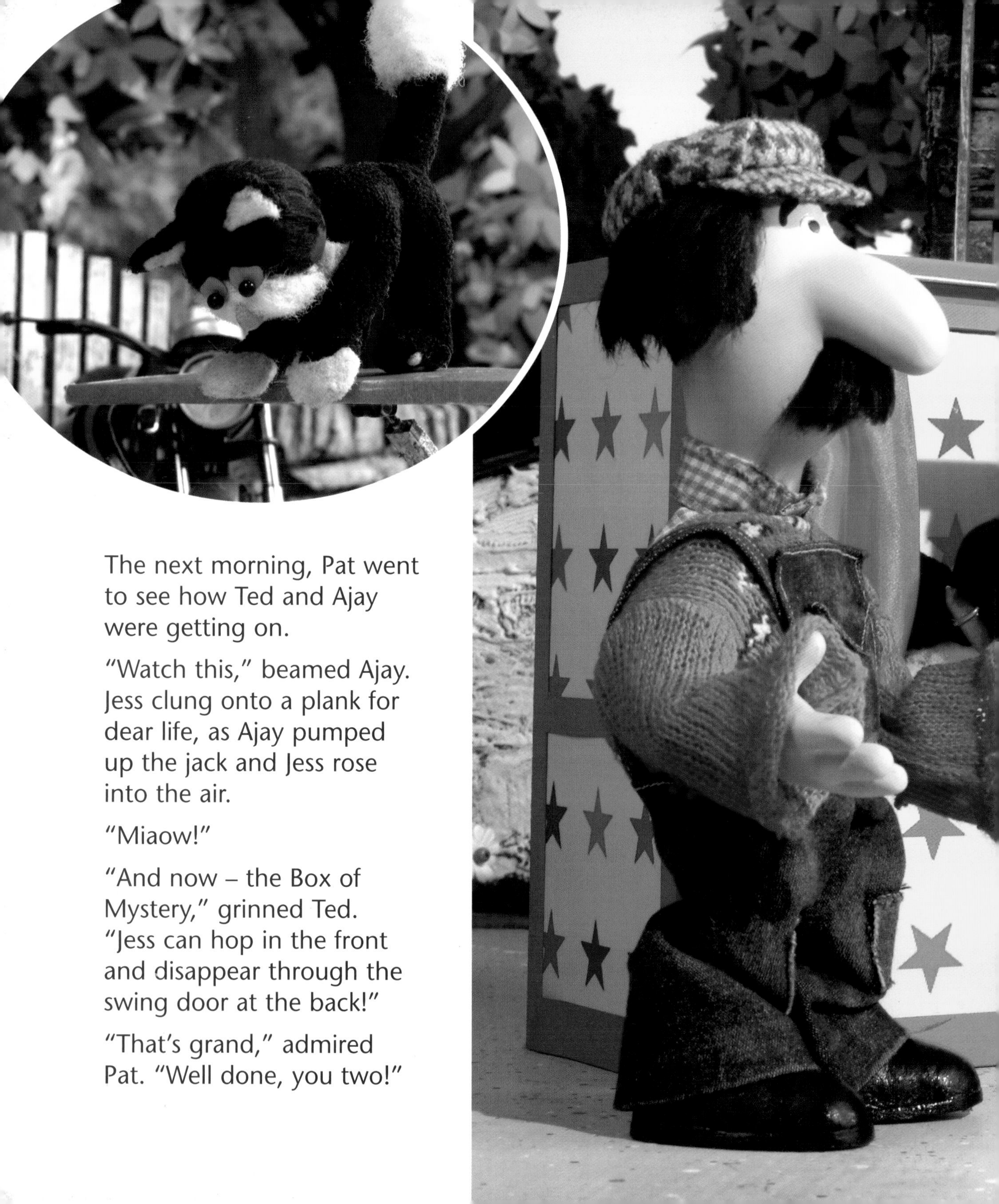

The next morning, Pat went to see how Ted and Ajay were getting on.

"Watch this," beamed Ajay. Jess clung onto a plank for dear life, as Ajay pumped up the jack and Jess rose into the air.

"Miaow!"

"And now – the Box of Mystery," grinned Ted. "Jess can hop in the front and disappear through the swing door at the back!"

"That's grand," admired Pat. "Well done, you two!"

The party was in full swing at the school hall. Meera and Julian were doing their best disco dancing.

"And now, quiet everyone!" announced Ajay.

"Please welcome the Amazing Patini!"

The crowd whistled and clapped.

"Ladies and gentlemen!" said Pat, making a bunch of flowers appear. "I'd like to wish Meera a very Happy Birthday!"

"And now, for my first trick. Lucy, pick a card!"

Julian looked worried as Pat chanted the magic words:

"With the magic that I've got, Your card will rise up to the top!

The nine of diamonds! Was that your card, Lucy?"

"Yes!" cried Lucy. Everyone cheered, especially Julian!

Then Pat dropped Lucy's card into his top hat, tapped his magic wand and pulled out . . . Nikhil's green rabbit!

There was a roar of applause.

"For my next trick, I need the birthday girl! Meera, please lie down on the magic carpet!

With this magic, you shall fly, Higher up towards the sky!"

There were gasps of astonishment as Meera slowly floated upwards. No one could see Ajay operating the jack from behind the curtain.

Meera floated gently back to the ground, and curtsied to the cheering audience.

"Thank you, Meera!"

"And for my final trick, I need the assistance of a black-and-white cat!"

"Miaow!" Jess jumped into the Box of Mystery.

Pat shut the curtain and waved his wand.

"Jess, my cat, my black-and-white cat.

My famous cat that we all know.

I command you, Jess, my black- and -white cat. . .

My black-and-white cat must go!"

Jess jumped out through the swing door and Pat and Meera opened the curtain to reveal the empty box!

While the audience applauded loudly, Nisha secretly coaxed Jess back into the box with a chicken leg.

"Miaow!" Jess leapt in to grab the chicken but then he leapt straight out again without Nisha noticing!

"Jess is white, Jess is black,
And now I command you,
Jess, come back!" chanted Pat.

But when Pat and Nisha drew back the curtain, there was no Jess!

Pat quickly shut the curtain again.

"Oh dear! Jess? Where are you?" he muttered.

There was no sign of him anywhere.

Then Ted peered into Pat's top hat. "By gum, look who's here, Pat!"

Pat grinned. "Ladies and gentlemen!" he announced. "I think Jess is ready to come back!

Jess is white and Jess is black,
I command you, Jess,
come back, come back!"

And out popped Jess from Pat's top hat. "Meee-iaow!"

"You are clever, Dad," said Julian, proudly.

"Wow, thanks, Pat," smiled Meera. "You've made my birthday . . . magic!"

Everyone applauded as the Amazing Patini took a bow!

SIMON AND SCHUSTER
First published in 2006 in Great Britain by Simon & Schuster UK Ltd
Africa House, 64-78 Kingsway
London WC2B 6AH

Original writer John Cunliffe
From the original television design by Ivor Wood

A CIP catalogue record for this book is available from the British Library upon request

ISBN 1416910557

Printed in China

1 3 5 7 9 10 8 6 4 2